The Rattlin' Bog

Ari Atarka

Hey! Ho! The Rattlin' Bog
The bog down in the valley-oh
Hey! Ho! The Rattlin' Bog
The bog down in the valley-oh

In that bog, there was a tree,
A rare tree, a Rattlin' tree.
And the tree in the bog,
And the bog down in the
Valley-oh!

Hey! Ho! The Rattlin' Bog
The bog down in the valley-oh
Hey! Ho! The Rattlin' Bog
The bog down in the valley-oh

On that tree, there was a door,
A rare door, a Rattlin' door.
And the door on the tree,
And the tree in the bog,
And the bog down in the
Valley-oh!

Hey! Ho! The Rattlin' Bog
The bog down in the valley-oh
Hey! Ho! The Rattlin' Bog
The bog down in the valley-oh

Past that door, there was a house,
A rare house, a Rattlin' house.
And the house part the door,
And the door on the tree,
And the tree in the bog,
And the bog down in the Valley-oh!

Hey! Ho! The Rattlin' Bog
The bog down in the valley-oh
Hey! Ho! The Rattlin' Bog
The bog down in the valley-oh

In that house, there was a gnome,
A rare gnome, a Rattlin' gnome.
And the gnome in the house,
And the house part the door,
And the door on the tree,
And the tree in the bog,
And the bog down in the Valley-oh!

Hey! Ho! The Rattlin' Bog
The bog down in the valley-oh
Hey! Ho! The Rattlin' Bog
The bog down in the valley-oh

On that gnome, there were some boots,
Some rare boots, some Rattlin' boots.
And the boots on the gnome,
And the gnome in the house,
And the house part the door,
And the door on the tree,
And the tree in the bog,
And the bog down in the
Valley-oh!

Hey! Ho! The Rattlin' Bog
The bog down in the valley-oh
Hey! Ho! The Rattlin' Bog
The bog down in the valley-oh

On those boots, there were some laces,
Some rare laces, some Rattlin' laces.
And the laces on the boots,
And the boots on the gnome,
And the gnome in the house,
And the house part the door,
And the door on the tree,
And the tree in the bog,
And the bog down in the
Valley-oh!

Hey! Ho! The Rattlin' Bog
The bog down in the valley-oh
Hey! Ho! The Rattlin' Bog
The bog down in the valley-oh

And on those laces,
There was an end!

The End

Rattlin' Bog

Irish Folk Song

Copyright © [2021] by [Ari Atarka]
All rights reserved
ISBN: 9798783129698
Imprint: Independently published

Printed in Great Britain
by Amazon